S0-AVW-736

TEAM SPIRIT®

SMART BOOKS FOR YOUNG FANS

THE BROOKLYN NETS

BY
MARK STEWART

NorwoodHouse Press
CHICAGO, ILLINOIS

Norwood House Press
P.O. Box 316598
Chicago, Illinois 60631

For information regarding Norwood House Press, please visit our website at:
www.norwoodhousepress.com or call 866-565-2900.

All photos courtesy of Associated Press except the following:
Macfadden Publishing/Bartell Media (6), Topps, Inc. (7, 18, 26, 27, 34 left, 35 all, 38, 42 left, 43 top),
Editions Rencontre (15, 28), The Star Company (21, 34 right, 45), Beckett Publications (22),
Capitol Card Co. (24), NY/NJ Nets (33, 42), Black Book Partners (37, 40), Basketball Digest (41).
Cover Photo: Matt York/Associated Press

The memorabilia and artifacts pictured in this book are presented for educational and informational purposes,
and come from the collection of the author.

Editor: Mike Kennedy
Designer: Ron Jaffe
Project Management: Black Book Partners, LLC.
Special thanks to Topps, Inc.

Library of Congress Cataloging-in-Publication Data

Stewart, Mark, 1960 July 7-
The Brooklyn Nets / by Mark Stewart.
pages cm. -- (Team spirit)
Includes bibliographical references and index.
Summary: "A revised Team Spirit Basketball edition featuring the Brooklyn Nets that chronicles the history and accomplishments of the team. Includes access to the Team Spirit website which provides additional information and photos"-- Provided by publisher.
ISBN 978-1-59953-637-8 (library edition : alk. paper) -- ISBN 978-1-60357-646-8 (ebook)
1. Brooklyn Nets (Basketball team)--History--Juvenile literature. I. Title.
GV885.52.B76S74 2014
796.323'640974723--dc23
2014006459

253N—072014
Manufactured in the United States of America in North Mankato, Minnesota.

COVER PHOTO: The Nets have given their fans thrilling moments everywhere they've called home, including Brooklyn.

Table of Contents

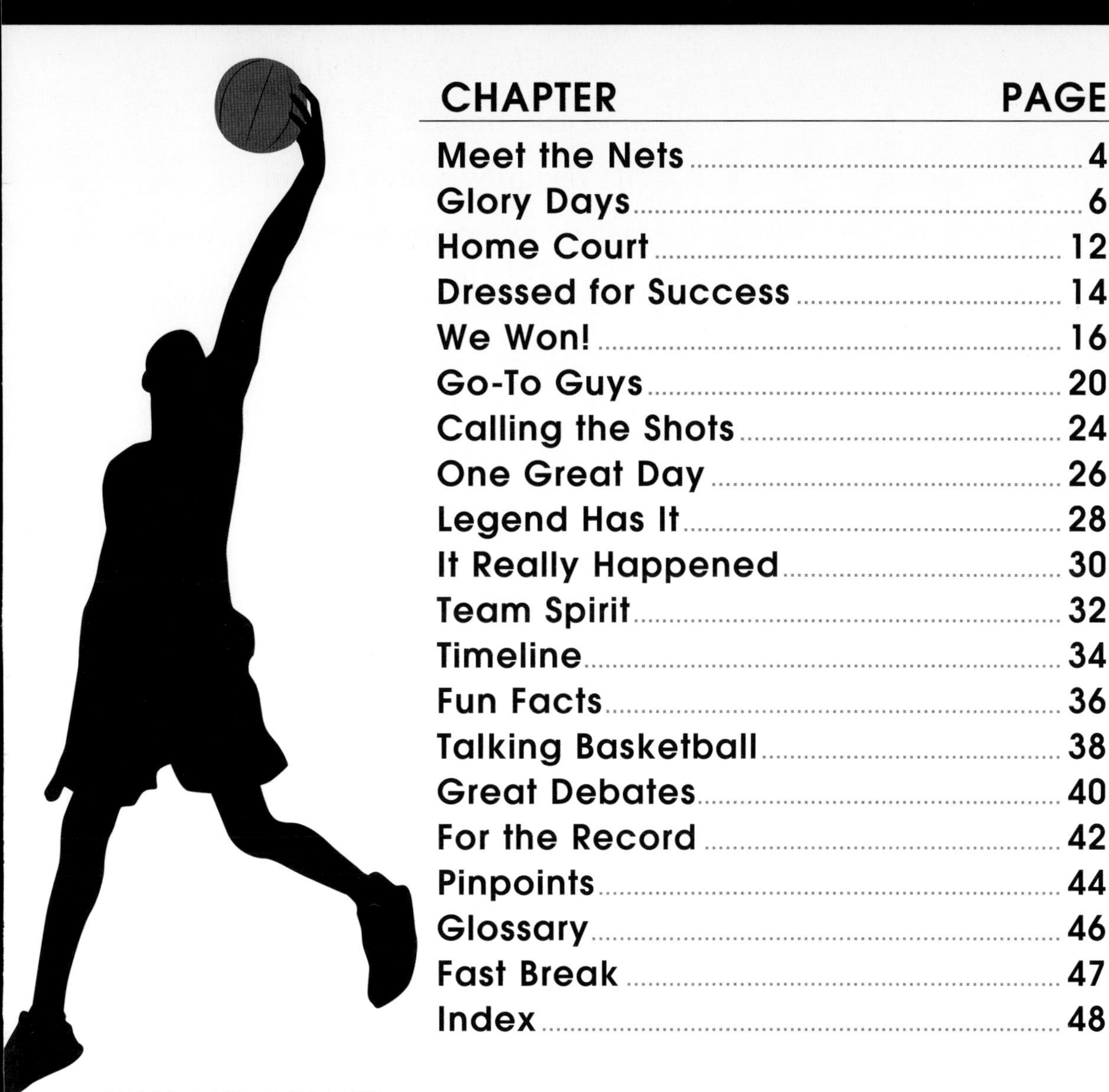

ABOUT OUR GLOSSARY

In this book, there may be several words that you are reading for the first time. Some are sports words, some are new vocabulary words, and some are familiar words that are used in an unusual way. All of these words are defined on page 46. Throughout the book, sports words appear in **bold type**. Regular vocabulary words appear in ***bold italic type***.

BROOKLYN
6
BROOKLYN
8
NETS
47
30

Meet the Nets

The game of basketball was invented more than 120 years ago in Springfield, Massachusetts. So why do some experts call Brooklyn, New York, the "cradle" of the sport? Perhaps it is because so many of the game's greats were born there and grew up on the neighborhood courts. Or maybe it's because some of the best coaches learned their craft on the playgrounds and in the gyms around the ***borough***. In 2012, the New Jersey Nets moved to Brooklyn and started to write a new chapter in basketball history.

Brooklyn is the team's eighth home. The Nets have played in four cities in New Jersey and three in New York. They have known incredible success and crushing disappointment. Win or lose, they have always played entertaining basketball.

This book tells the story of the Nets. They have had some of basketball's greatest stars and been part of many unforgettable moments. They have traveled a long and bumpy road, but it has been worth it. Brooklyn finally feels like home.

Deron Williams raises a fist to celebrate a victory during the 2013–14 season.

Glory Days

Is New York City big enough for two ***professional*** basketball teams? In 1967, Arthur Brown decided to find out. He bought a team in the **American Basketball Association (ABA)** and looked for an arena in Manhattan. He wanted to go head-to-head with the New York Knicks of the **National Basketball Association (NBA)**.

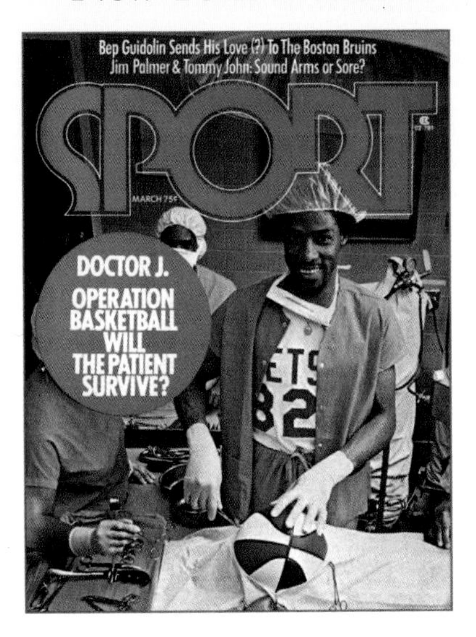

When the NBA prevented him from renting an arena, Brown moved his team to Teaneck, New Jersey, and named it the Americans.

Like most ABA teams, the Americans were made up of overlooked or unwanted players. Their best player, Tony Jackson, had actually been banned from the NBA. Many years earlier, his name had come up in a gambling scandal. Although Jackson was never charged with a crime, the NBA still outlawed him. By contrast, the ABA gave second chances to many talented players.

In 1968–69, the Americans moved to Long Island, New York, and changed their name to the Nets. By the early 1970s, the Nets had a very good team. Forward Rick Barry, guard Bill Melchionni, and center Billy Paultz formed the core. They led the Nets to the **ABA Finals** in the spring of 1972.

Julius Erving joined the Nets for the 1973–74 season. "Dr. J" was a spectacular player who captured the imagination of basketball fans everywhere. With the help of three young stars—John Williamson, Larry Kenon, and Brian Taylor—Erving led the Nets to the ABA championship. Two years later, New York won a second title. The 1976 ABA Finals turned out to be the last games the league played. The following season, the Nets and three other ABA teams were invited to join the NBA. The ABA went out of business.

Hoping to make a splash in their first NBA season, the Nets traded for point guard Nate "Tiny" Archibald. When he teamed up with Erving, the Nets instantly became championship **contenders**. Unfortunately, this plan fell apart. Short on cash, the Nets had no choice but to sell Erving, and then Archibald injured his ankle and was lost for the year. New York finished in last place, and few fans came to watch the team play.

LEFT: Julius Erving liked to have fun with his nickname.
ABOVE: Bill Melchionni was one of the team's early stars.

NET
5
ROBINSON
50

The Nets moved to New Jersey prior to the 1977–78 season. They hoped more fans would come to see them in their new home. By the early 1980s, the Nets had a number of good players, including Buck Williams, Otis Birdsong, Albert King, Darryl Dawkins, Mike Gminski, and Micheal Ray Richardson. Starting in 1981–82, they made it to the **playoffs** five years in a row.

In the 1990s, the Nets found new stars in Derrick Coleman, Jayson Williams, Sam Bowie, Mookie Blaylock, Drazen Petrovic, and Kenny Anderson. New Jersey went to the playoffs four times but never advanced beyond the first round. Tragedy struck when Petrovic died in a car crash. The team struggled to recover from this devastating blow.

In 2001–02, the Nets were ready again to challenge for the NBA championship. Things turned around when Jason Kidd joined the team. The **All-Star** point guard helped mold talented players Kenyon Martin, Kerry Kittles, Lucious Harris, Richard Jefferson, and Keith Van Horn into an excellent team. The Nets improved to 52 wins and made it all the way to the **NBA Finals**. The following year, they returned to the NBA Finals. Unfortunately, New Jersey lost both times.

LEFT: Jason Kidd drives to the hoop for a layup.
ABOVE: Jayson Williams starred for the team in the 1990s.

The Nets continued adding talented players to their roster, including All-Star Vince Carter. They finished atop their **division** four times in five seasons. However, New Jersey could not take the final step and win the NBA championship.

In 2008, Kidd asked to be traded. He was nearing the end of his career and wanted to play for a club that he could push over the top. The Nets sent him to the Dallas Mavericks and received a group of players and **draft picks** in return. As Kidd guided Dallas to its first NBA championship, New Jersey began to rebuild.

Before the 2009–10 season, the team was purchased by a Russian billionaire named Mikhail Prokhorov. He announced that he would move the Nets back to New York—to the borough of Brooklyn—where they would play in a spectacular new arena. Prokhorov also promised he would spare no expense in building the Nets into a championship contender. His plan was to make the Nets a team with ***international*** popularity.

The Nets traded for Deron Williams and Joe Johnson, two of the league's best guards. They added Paul Pierce and Kevin Garnett in a deal with the Boston Celtics. They also signed forward Andrei Kirilenko. Along with center Brook Lopez, this group formed the core of a competitive team. They were coached by a familiar face, as Kidd made his return to the Nets. There was pressure to create a winning ***tradition*** in Brooklyn right way. The Nets were ready for the challenge.

LEFT: Vince Carter averaged more than 23 points a game for the Nets.
ABOVE: Kevin Garnett and Paul Pierce brought valuable championship experience to Brooklyn.

a world of entertainment and sports.
americanexpress.com/entertainment
61
Tribe
ATL
4
ATL
3
ATL
0
NBA

Home Court

It should come as no surprise that the Nets have called eight different arenas home. Their longest stay anywhere was nine years in the Meadowlands Sports Complex in New Jersey. For most of their time in Long Island, the Nets played at the Nassau Coliseum.

In 2012, the Nets moved into a newly constructed arena in Brooklyn. It was built on the spot where the Dodgers baseball team had wanted to move in the 1950s. The arena is one of the most modern in sports. Fans also love it because every seat makes them feel like they are right in the middle of the action.

BY THE NUMBERS

- *The Nets' arena has 17,732 seats for basketball.*
- *The arena can be reached by 11 subway lines, 11 bus lines, and the Long Island Railroad.*
- *As of 2013–14, the Nets had retired seven numbers: 3 (Drazen Petrovic), 4 (Wendell Ladner), 5 (Jason Kidd), 23 (John Williamson), 25 (Bill Melchionni), 32 (Julius Erving), and 52 (Buck Williams).*

Joe Johnson floats to the rim during a 2013–14 home game. Nets fans get great views in the team's new arena.

BROOKLYN
34
NETS

Dressed for Success

For most of their history, the Nets used red, white, and blue as their colors. They often had *Nets* written across the front of their jerseys. In 1972, while still in the ABA, the team introduced a uniform design with stars. When the Nets moved to Brooklyn, they changed their colors to black and white. But the team also paid respect to the past by creating a uniform with a star pattern.

The team ***logo*** has changed a lot over the years, too. It had always recognized the team's home state, whether it was New York or New Jersey. The current logo instead proudly displays a *B* for Brooklyn inside a basketball.

LEFT: Paul Pierce jogs down the court in the team's 2013–14 home uniform. The Brooklyn logo can be seen on his shorts.
ABOVE: Nate Archibald wears the uniform from the Nets' early NBA days.

We Won!

Since moving from the ABA in 1976, the Nets have reached the NBA Finals twice. Their first trip to the championship series came in 2001–02, after they finished with the best record in the **Eastern Conference**. The Nets opened the playoffs by defeating the Indiana Pacers and then the Charlotte Hornets (now the New Orleans Pelicans). Their next opponent, the Boston Celtics, gave them all they could handle.

The series was very physical from the start. At one point, Jason Kidd needed 32 stitches to close a gash over his eye. The Nets closed out the Celtics in Game 6, thanks in part to a **3-pointer** by Keith Van Horn in the fourth quarter. Kenyon Martin ripped off his jersey and strutted around the arena after the victory. Unfortunately, the Nets lost four straight to the Los Angeles Lakers in the NBA Finals.

The following season, the Nets made another run at the championship. Their road to the NBA Finals was easier this time. They beat the Milwaukee Bucks in six games, and then swept the

Kenyon Martin throws down a dunk during the 2002 NBA Finals.

Celtics and Detroit Pistons to win their second Eastern Conference crown. In the NBA Finals, they faced the San Antonio Spurs. The teams split the first four games, giving Nets fans hope that their first NBA title was within reach. But the Spurs took control in Game 6, and then won the championship with a great performance in Game 7.

Despite the painful losses in 2002 and 2003, two championship banners hang from the rafters in the team's home in Brooklyn. Both came during the Nets' years in the ABA. They captured their first title in 1973–74. Prior to the season, the Nets made a trade with the Virginia Squires that brought league scoring champion Julius Erving to the team. Erving joined a talented supporting cast that included guards Brian Taylor and John Williamson, forward Larry Kenon, and center Billy Paultz. They might have been the best starting five in all of basketball that season. Mike Gale and Wendell Ladner were great off the bench.

In the 1974 playoffs, Erving led the Nets to victory over his old team in five games. Next, the Nets defeated the powerful Kentucky Colonels in four games. The Colonels had two of the best big men in the ABA, Artis Gilmore and Dan Issel. Erving won Game 3 with a fade-away jump shot that banked in at the buzzer.

The ABA Finals gave the Nets their greatest challenge. The Utah Stars had five good starters who matched up well with the Nets. Nevertheless, New York won the first two games at home, and then beat the Stars in **overtime** in Game 3. After dropping the next contest, the Nets won Game 5 for their first championship.

Two years later, Erving won his third scoring title and led the Nets back to the ABA Finals. Paultz and Kenon had moved on, but the team got solid seasons from newcomers Al Skinner and Rich Jones. The Nets outlasted the Spurs in the semifinals to set up a showdown with the Denver Nuggets.

Erving and David Thompson of the Nuggets were the most exciting players in basketball. They put on a show for six games,

but in the end the Nets won out. Denver put up a good fight in the clincher, building a huge lead in the second half. But the Nets turned it on in the fourth quarter. They played amazing defense, using a **full-court press** that completely confused the Nuggets. Meanwhile, Erving, Williamson, and center Jim Eakins made big baskets down the stretch. The Nets won for their second ABA title. It was the last ABA game ever played—and, many believe, the greatest one in league history.

LEFT: This trading card shows the 1974 ABA champs.
ABOVE: Julius Erving lifts his arms in triumph as the Nets clinch their 1976 ABA championship.

Go-To Guys

To be a true star in the NBA, you need more than a great shot. You have to be a "go-to guy"—someone teammates trust to make the winning play when the seconds are ticking away in a big game. Nets fans have had a lot to cheer about over the years, including these great stars …

THE PIONEERS

BILLY PAULTZ — 6′ 11″ Center

• BORN: 7/30/1948 • PLAYED FOR TEAM: 1970–71 TO 1974–75

Billy Paultz was big and smart, and very difficult to guard. In fact, he was nicknamed the "Whopper" because he was so hard to handle. Paultz averaged double-figures in scoring and rebounding with the Nets.

RICK BARRY — 6′ 7″ Forward

• BORN: 3/28/1944 • PLAYED FOR TEAM: 1970–71 TO 1971–72

Rick Barry was one of the greatest shooters in basketball history. He scored more than 4,000 points in his two seasons with the Nets and led them to the ABA Finals in the spring of 1972. Many fans remember Barry for his underhanded shooting style at the foul line.

JULIUS ERVING 6′ 7″ Forward

• Born: 2/22/1950 • Played for Team: 1973–74 to 1975–76

Julius Erving was the ABA's most exciting and talented player. Dr. J averaged more than 28 points a game with the Nets. He was the ABA **Most Valuable Player (MVP)** twice and co-MVP once, and guided the Nets to two ABA titles.

JOHN WILLIAMSON 6′ 2″ Guard

• Born: 11/10/1951 • Died: 11/30/1996

• Played for Team: 1973–74 to 1975–76 & 1977–78 to 1978–79

"Super John" Williamson loved to live up to this nickname. No matter what the defense tried, he always found a way to get an open shot. As a **rookie**, Williamson helped the Nets win their first championship.

OTIS BIRDSONG 6′ 4″ Guard

• Born: 12/9/1955

• Played for Team: 1981–82 to 1987–88

Otis Birdsong helped turn the Nets into a winner during the 1980s. The team reached the playoffs five years in a row after he arrived. Birdsong gave the Nets good scoring, passing, and defense.

BUCK WILLIAMS 6′ 8″ Forward

• Born: 3/8/1960 • Played for Team: 1981–82 to 1988–89

Few players worked as hard as Buck Williams did. The year he joined the Nets, they improved by 20 victories. Williams was one of the NBA's top three rebounders six times during the 1980s.

ABOVE: Otis Birdsong

DERRICK COLEMAN

6′ 10″ Forward

• BORN: 6/21/1967

• PLAYED FOR TEAM: 1990–91 TO 1994–95

Derrick Coleman was a powerful rebounder with a smooth scoring touch. He was named **Rookie of the Year** in his first season with the Nets. He averaged just under 20 points a game during his career in New Jersey.

JAYSON WILLIAMS 6′ 9″ Forward

• BORN: 2/22/1968

• PLAYED FOR TEAM: 1992–93 TO 1998–99

Jayson Williams loved to play basketball, and it showed. With the Nets, he became a team leader and an All-Star. Williams was one of the NBA's top rebounders before a collision with a teammate ended his career.

RICHARD JEFFERSON 6′ 7″ Forward

• BORN: 3/23/1973 • PLAYED FOR TEAM: 2001–02 TO 2007–08

Richard Jefferson was viewed as a role player when he joined the Nets. He worked hard and became one of the team's most valuable starters. Jefferson was at his best driving to the basket for power dunks.

ABOVE: Derrick Coleman **RIGHT**: Brook Lopez

JASON KIDD 6′ 4″ Guard

- BORN: 3/23/1973
- PLAYED FOR TEAM: 2001–02 TO 2007–08

The Nets took a risk when they traded for Jason Kidd. He showed he was worth it by providing great leadership. Kidd's all-around game made him the league's most dazzling point guard. He returned to coach the Nets in 2013–14.

BROOK LOPEZ 7′ 0″ Center

- BORN: 6/29/1981
- FIRST SEASON WITH TEAM: 2008–09

The Nets selected Brook Lopez with the 10th pick in the 2008 NBA draft. Each season with the team, he found a way to improve. In 2012–13, Lopez made the All-Star team. A year later, he was off to a great start before an injury ended his season.

DERON WILLIAMS 6′ 3″ Guard

- BORN: 6/26/1984
- FIRST YEAR WITH TEAM: 2010–11

The Nets traded two good players, two first-round draft picks, and $3 million for Deron Williams. That pressure never seemed to bother him. Williams was an All-Star in his first two seasons with the Nets.

Calling the Shots

Few teams can match the Nets when it comes to hiring quality coaches. Though the team has played fewer than 50 seasons, some of the most famous names in pro basketball have called the shots for the Nets. Among the most notable were Max Zaslofsky, Larry Brown, Willis Reed, Chuck Daly, and Bill Fitch. Among the most successful were Lou Carnesecca, Kevin Loughery, and Byron Scott.

Carnesecca coached the Nets during their ABA days. He was known for his great sense of humor, which helped his players relax and do their best. Carnesecca also liked to wear wild and colorful sweaters. He led the Nets to the ABA Finals in 1972. Loughery took over the team in 1973. He was a tough and talkative coach who built a great team around his star player, Julius Erving. Under Loughery, the Nets won two ABA championships. He coached the club in its first five years in the NBA.

In 2002 and 2003, Scott led the Nets to the NBA Finals. As a player, Scott was a key member of the Los Angeles Lakers during their championship years in the 1980s. He coached the Nets to attack the basket and play tough defense. Working with ***veteran*** Jason Kidd, Scott molded a collection of young talent into a championship contender. His biggest challenge was convincing the Nets that they could be winners. Having Kidd on the floor helped the team believe it could win any game.

After the Nets moved to Brooklyn, owner Mikhail Prokhorov wanted to build a winning team as quickly as possible. He spent millions on superstars such as Joe Johnson, Kevin Garnett, and Paul Pierce. And who better to coach the team than the recently retired Kidd? Although Kidd had no coaching experience, Prokhorov believed he was the only man for the job.

LEFT: This trading card of Lou Carnesecca includes one of his famous sweaters.
ABOVE: Kevin Loughery gives instructions to the Nets.

One Great Day

MAY 13, 1976

When the Nets and Denver Nuggets took the floor for Game 6 of the 1976 ABA Finals, both teams knew that the league was doomed. A deal had already been made for four ABA teams (including the Nets and Nuggets) to join the NBA. The Nets had the lead in the series. They were hoping to make this game the last one played in ABA history.

Desperate to force a seventh game, the Nuggets focused on controlling Julius Erving. They built a 22-point lead late in the third quarter, and seemed to have the game locked up. That's when Dr. J started to operate. Each time down the court, he took the ball and attacked the defense until he drew a double-team. The moment the second defender came to him, Erving whipped the ball to an open teammate. As Denver scrambled to recover, the Nets kept passing until the Nuggets were in total disarray. Slowly but surely, they chipped away at the Denver lead.

With the Nuggets starting to panic, John Williamson took over. Super John went wild in the fourth quarter and scored 16 points. The Nets rode his hot hand and blew past the Nuggets. When the clock ran out, they celebrated a 112–106 victory and their second ABA championship.

Brian Taylor, the Nets' point guard, still uses this amazing comeback to explain the importance of teamwork. "It helps me when I'm teaching kids about overcoming adversity," Taylor says. "We overcame adversity in a very short period of time, but it's a life lesson for us."

LEFT: Super John Williamson lived up to his nickname in the fourth quarter against Denver. **ABOVE**: Brian Taylor learned a great deal from the Nets' comeback victory.

Legend Has It

Has a player ever worn both teams' uniforms in the same game?

LEGEND HAS IT that three have. During the 1978–79 season, the Nets lost a game to the Philadelphia 76ers. Afterwards, the NBA realized the referees had made a mistake in the third quarter. The league ordered the game to be replayed from that point. In the meantime, the Nets and 76ers made a trade. Ralph Simpson and Harvey Catchings—who were 76ers at the start of the game—would finish the game with the Nets. Eric Money, who began the game as a Net, would finish it as a 76er. All three players appeared in the official score sheet for both teams.

ABOVE: The back of this trading card tells the strange story of the trade between the Nets and 76ers. The front shows Eric Money taking a shot for Philadelphia.

Did Nets fans experience "déjà vu" in 2008?

LEGEND HAS IT that they did. *Déjà vu* is a French saying that means "already seen." In 2001, the Nets drafted center Jason Collins out of Stanford University. Collins had a twin brother who played at Stanford and was also drafted that spring. In 2008, the Nets drafted center Brook Lopez out of Stanford University. Just like Collins, Lopez had a twin brother who played at Stanford and was also drafted that spring.

Were the Nets once whistled for eight technical fouls on one play?

LEGEND HAS IT that they were. In an ABA game, Nets coach Kevin Loughery believed the Virginia Squires were playing an illegal **zone defense**. When the referees did not see it his way, Loughery ordered his players to line up in a zone defense of their own in protest. When the referees stopped the game, Loughery and his players began arguing. Eight technical fouls were called before order was restored.

It Really Happened

The Nets have played some close games over the years. However, no game was closer—or more exciting—than a playoff battle with the Indiana Pacers in 2002. The teams were tied at two wins each in their series. The winner of Game 5 would keep playing and the loser would go home for the summer.

It had been nearly 20 years since the Nets had won a series in the playoffs. They had fire in their eyes to start the game. No player was more focused than Kenyon Martin. Jason Kidd had challenged him the day before to play better. Martin responded with an amazing effort.

The only problem was that Indiana was equally intense. Every time New Jersey took a lead, the Pacers fought back. The teams were tied at halftime and at the end of the third quarter. Then, with the Nets up by three points, Reggie Miller banked in a 39-foot shot at the buzzer to tie the game.

In overtime, the Pacers went ahead, but Kidd brought the Nets back. He made two baskets and then passed to Martin for

Jason Kidd waves to the fans after the Nets' amazing victory over the Pacers.

a dunk. The game moved into a second overtime period. Kidd hit a jumper with two minutes left to give the Nets the lead, and they finally pulled away for a 120–109 victory. Kidd finished with 31 points. Martin, who played 56 minutes, scored 29. The two hugged each other after the game ended.

"We stuck it out and it showed how bad we wanted it," said Martin. The Nets did not stop there. They won their next two series to make it to the NBA Finals for the first time in team history.

Team Spirit

When the Nets moved from New Jersey to Brooklyn, they hoped to attract a new ***legion*** of fans. That happened almost immediately, as New Yorkers welcomed the chance to root for a new pro team. By the 2013–14 season, the team was selling out nearly every home game. Going to a Nets game had become one of the hottest tickets around.

One of the Nets' biggest supporters is hip-hop star Jay–Z. In 2004, he purchased part of the team, and later played a key role in the team's move to Brooklyn. He and his wife, Beyoncé, can often be seen watching Nets games from their courtside seats.

LEFT: Jay-Z and Beyoncé like to be close to the action at Nets games.
ABOVE: Nets fans bought this yearbook during the team's fourth ABA season.

Timeline

The basketball season is played from October through June. That means each season takes place at the end of one year and the beginning of the next. In this timeline, the accomplishments of the Americans and Nets are shown by season.

1973–74
The Nets win their first ABA championship.

1976–77
The Nets join the NBA.

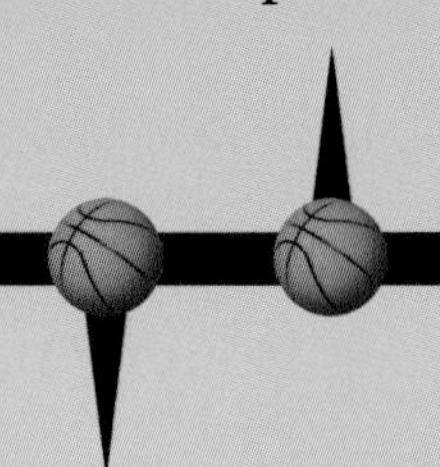

1967–68
The team plays its first season as the New Jersey Americans.

1975–76
The Nets win their second ABA championship.

1982–83
Micheal Ray Richardson leads the NBA in steals per game.

Billy Paultz starred for the team in the 1960s.

Micheal Ray Richardson's nickname was "Sugar."

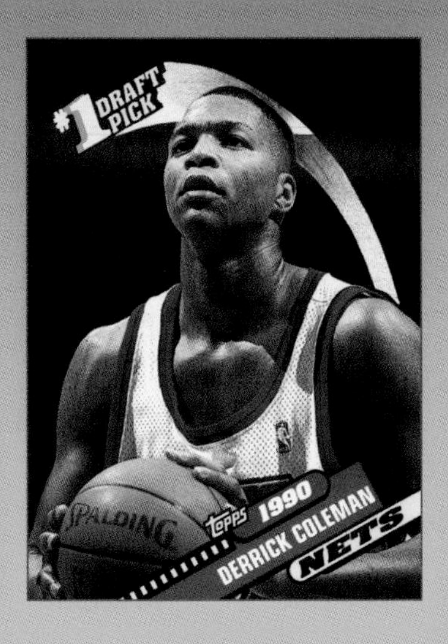

Derrick Coleman

Brook Lopez

2001–02
The Nets reach the NBA Finals for the first time.

1990–91
Derrick Coleman is named Rookie of the Year.

2008–09
Brook Lopez makes the **All-Rookie Team**.

1993–94
Kenny Anderson starts in the All-Star Game.

2002–03
The Nets return to the NBA Finals.

2012–13
The Nets move to Brooklyn.

Richard Jefferson was a key contributor in 2001–02 and 2002–03.

Fun Facts

YOU AGAIN?

During the 2007–08 season, Jason Kidd recorded a **triple-double** in three games against the Charlotte Bobcats. The last player with three triple-doubles against the same team was Magic Johnson, 18 years earlier.

STOLEN MOMENT

Early in the 1985–86 season, the Nets defeated the Indiana Pacers in a wild triple-overtime game, 147–138. Micheal Ray Richardson had 38 points, 11 rebounds, 11 assists, and nine steals. Had Richardson made one more steal he would have become just the second player in history at that time with an official **quadruple-double**.

NO ORDINARY JOE

When the Nets traded for Joe Johnson from the Atlanta Hawks, he made it clear he was happy to be in Brooklyn. In his favorite video game, NBA 2K, Johnson would only take the court as the Nets.

GAME OF THRONES

Two of the Nets' greatest players were brothers: Bernard and Albert King. Bernard was the team's first star after the Nets moved to New Jersey. The Kings ruled for eight seasons—Albert for six and Bernard for two.

EASTERN BLOCK

Each year from 2002 to 2004, the Nets chose a young Eastern European star with their first pick in the NBA draft—Nenad Krstic (Serbia), Zoran Planinic (Croatia), and Viktor Khryapa (Russia).

SWAT TEAM

The Nets won just 24 games in 1977–78, but no team in the NBA blocked more shots. New Jersey had 560 in all. Center George Johnson led the league with 274.

ABOVE: Bernard King muscles his way toward the basket. He was one of the Nets' two Kings.

Talking Basketball

"I had a wonderful experience with the Nets playing for Louie Carnesecca."

▶ **Rick Barry,** *on his two seasons in New York*

"I try to get control of the flow, and get my teammates the ball in the best position to score."

▶ **Deron Williams,** *on his main job as a point guard*

"I have so much respect for him. I've known Jason since I've been in the NBA and I think he's just a natural born leader."

▶ **Paul Pierce,** *on Jason Kidd*

“Passing is ***contagious.*** There’s nothing better than making the pass that gives someone an easy hoop.”

► **Jason Kidd,** *on what made him a great point guard*

“It’s all about winning. There are no ***egos.*** Check your egos at the door. We’re out there to win.”

► **Brook Lopez,** *on what a team of stars must do to succeed*

“I wanted to undertake the challenge of daring to be great.”

► **Julius Erving,** *on what made him a superstar*

“We had the right system to be successful. We just had to find the right players for the system, and we were able to do that.”

► **Byron Scott,** *on building the Nets into a championship contender*

LEFT: Rick Barry
ABOVE: Jason Kidd

Great Debates

People who root for the Nets love to compare their favorite moments, teams, and players. Some debates have been going on for years! How would you settle these classic basketball arguments?

Derrick Coleman was the team's best power forward . . .

... because he was a great scorer and rebounder, and that's what a power forward is supposed to do. Coleman played five years with the Nets. In three of those seasons, he averaged more than 20 points and 10 rebounds a game. Coleman also played with a mean streak. Opponents hated matching up against him.

No way! Buck Williams played the position better than any Net . . .

... because he not only scored and rebounded, but he was a great defender, too. Williams (LEFT) played every game as if it were his last. He stayed on the floor until the coach practically had to drag him off. In his first seven seasons with the Nets, he averaged at least 15 points and 11 rebounds a game. In 1983–84, he led the NBA with 355 offensive rebounds.

The 2002-03 Nets would have beaten the 1975-76 Nets . . .

... because they had better athletes and a stronger bench. Kenyon Martin, Jason Collins, and Richard Jefferson would have controlled the boards. Jason Kidd would have run Brian Taylor into the ground. Kerry Kittles would have stayed a step ahead of John Williamson. With all those advantages, the 2002–03 Nets would have won easily.

Wait. What? The 1975-76 Nets would have totally destroyed them . . .

... because of Julius Erving (RIGHT). No one on the 2002–03 team could have stopped Dr. J. Erving was an unselfish player who loved to create open shots for his teammates. And the 1975–76 Nets could definitely knock down open shots. Even without Dr. J's help, the backcourt duo of Williamson and Taylor would have loved running with the 2002–03 Nets. That was their favorite style of play.

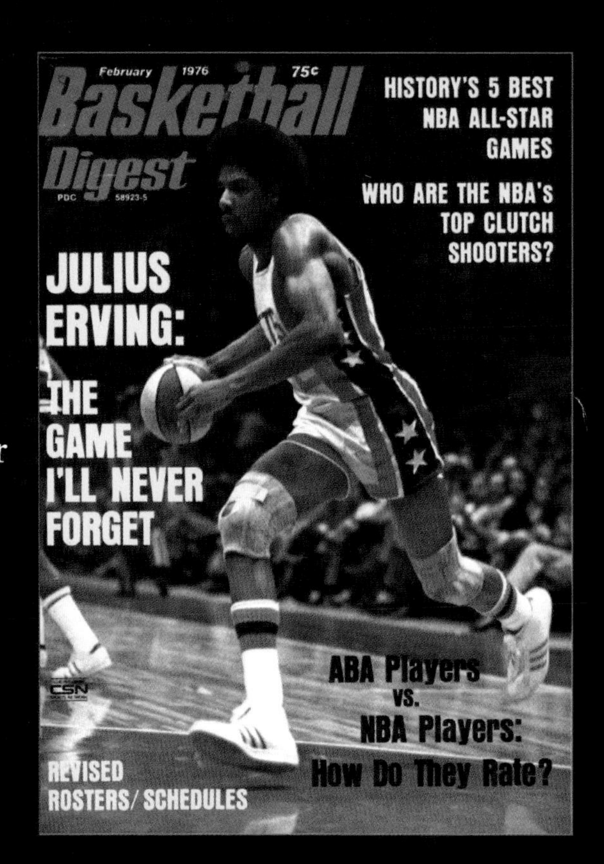

For the Record

The great Nets teams and players have left their marks on the record books. These are the "best of the best" …

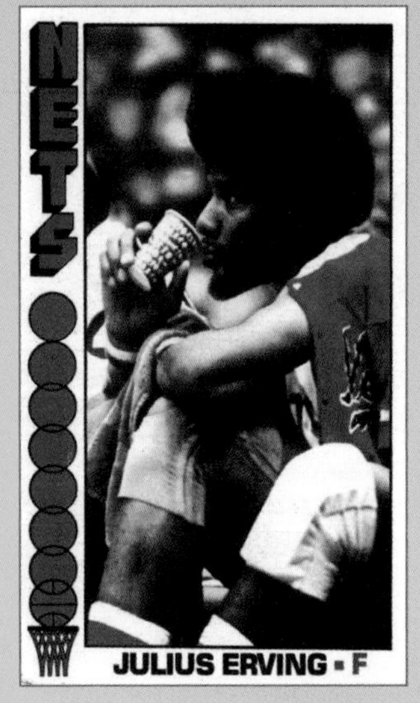

Julius Erving was the leader of the Nets in the 1970s. He was MVP of the ABA Finals twice.

NETS AWARD WINNERS

NBA ROOKIE OF THE YEAR	
Buck Williams	1981–82
Derrick Coleman	1990–91

ABA MVP	
Julius Erving	1973–74
Julius Erving	1974–75*

ABA FINALS MVP	
Julius Erving	1973–74
Julius Erving	1975–76

ABA SLAM DUNK CHAMPION	
Julius Erving	1975–76

ABA ROOKIE OF THE YEAR	
Brian Taylor	1972–73

** Shared award with another player.*

Nets fans bought this pennant to celebrate the team's 2003 Eastern Conference championship.

NETS ACHIEVEMENTS

ACHIEVEMENT	SEASON
ABA Eastern Division Champions	1973–74
ABA Champions	1973–74
ABA Champions	1975–76
Atlantic Division Champions	2001–02
Eastern Conference Champions	2001–02
Atlantic Division Champions	2002–03
Eastern Conference Champions	2002–03
Atlantic Division Champions	2003–04
Atlantic Division Champions	2005–06

Wendell Ladner was an ABA All-Star twice before joining the Nets. He played an important supporting role for the 1974 champs.

Richard Jefferson stretches for a powerful dunk. He helped the Nets win two conference championships.

Pinpoints

The history of a basketball team is made up of many smaller stories. These stories take place all over the map—not just in the city a team calls "home." Match the pushpins on these maps to the **TEAM FACTS**, and you will begin to see the story of the Nets unfold!

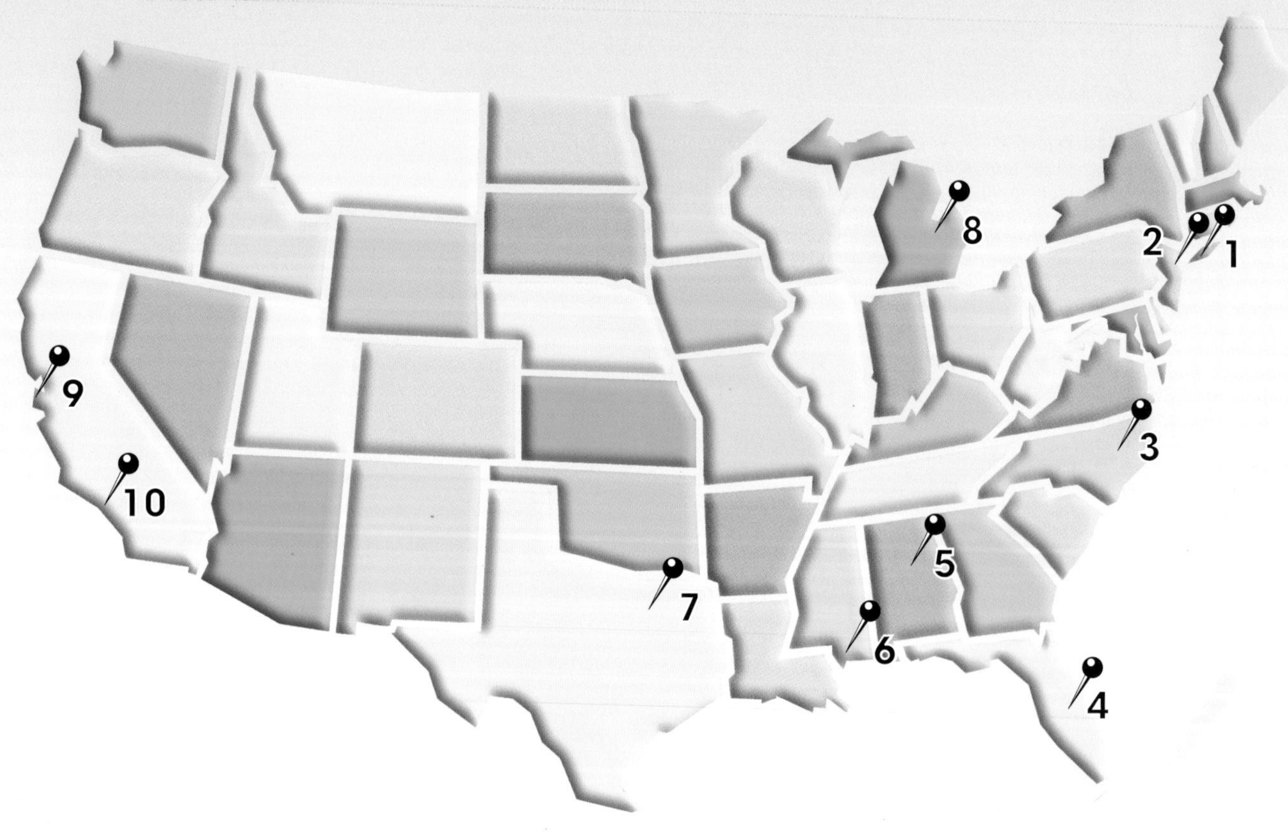

TEAM FACTS

1. Brooklyn, New York—*The Nets began playing here in 2012.*
2. East Rutherford, New Jersey—*The Nets played here from 1981 to 2011.*
3. Rocky Mount, North Carolina—*Buck Williams was born here.*
4. Orlando, Florida—*Darryl Dawkins was born here.*
5. Birmingham, Alabama—*Larry Kenon was born here.*
6. Necaise Crossing, Mississippi—*Wendell Ladner was born here.*
7. Garland, Texas—*Mookie Blaylock was born here.*
8. Saginaw, Michigan—*Kenyon Martin was born here.*
9. San Francisco, California—*Jason Kidd was born here.*
10. North Hollywood, California—*Brook Lopez was born here.*
11. Sibenik, Croatia—*Drazen Petrovic was born here.*
12. Izhevsk, Russia—*Andrei Kirilenko was born here.*

Darryl Dawkins

Glossary

Basketball Words
Vocabulary Words

3-POINTER—A basket made from behind the 3-point line.

ABA FINALS—The playoff series that decided the ABA champion.

ALL-ROOKIE TEAM—The annual honor given to the NBA's best first-year players at each position.

ALL-STAR—A player selected to play in the annual All-Star Game.

AMERICAN BASKETBALL ASSOCIATION (ABA)—The basketball league that played for nine seasons starting in 1967.

BOROUGH—One of the five subdivisions that make up New York City.

CONTAGIOUS—Likely to spread and affect others.

CONTENDERS—People who compete for a championship.

DIVISION—A group of teams within a league that play in the same part of the country.

DRAFT PICKS—Players selected or "drafted" by NBA teams each summer.

EASTERN CONFERENCE—A group of teams that play in the East. The winner of the Eastern Conference meets the winner of the Western Conference in the league finals.

EGOS—People's sense of self-importance.

FULL-COURT PRESS—A defensive game plan in which a team pressures the opponent for the entire length of the court.

INTERNATIONAL—From all over the world.

LEGION—A large number of people.

LOGO—A symbol or design that represents a company or team.

MOST VALUABLE PLAYER (MVP)—The annual award given to a league's best player; also given to the best player in the league finals and All-Star Game. The NBA also hands out MVP awards.

NATIONAL BASKETBALL ASSOCIATION (NBA)—The professional league that has been operating since 1946–47.

NBA FINALS—The playoff series that decides the champion of the league.

OVERTIME—The extra period played when a game is tied after 48 minutes.

PLAYOFFS—The games played after the season to determine the league champion.

PROFESSIONAL—A player or team that plays a sport for money.

QUADRUPLE-DOUBLE—A game in which a player records double-figures in four different statistical categories.

ROOKIE—A player in his first season.

ROOKIE OF THE YEAR—The annual award given to the league's best first-year player.

TRADITION—A belief or custom that is handed down from generation to generation.

TRIPLE-DOUBLE—A game in which a player records double-figures in three different statistical categories.

VETERAN—A player with great experience.

ZONE DEFENSE—A defense in which players are responsible for guarding an area of the court rather than covering a specific offensive player.

FAST BREAK

TEAM SPIRIT introduces a great way to stay up to date with your team! Visit our **FAST BREAK** link and get connected to the latest and greatest updates. **FAST BREAK** serves as a young reader's ticket to an exclusive web page—with more stories, fun facts, team records, and photos of the Nets. Content is updated during and after each season. The **FAST BREAK** feature also enables readers to send comments and letters to the author! Log onto:

www.norwoodhousepress.com/library.aspx

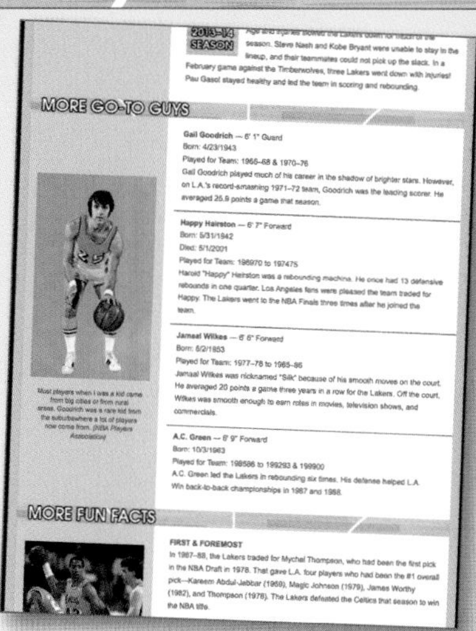

2013–14 SEASON
season. Steve Nash and Kobe Bryant were unable to stay in the lineup, and their teammates could not pick up the slack. In a February game against the Timberwolves, three Lakers went down with injuries! Pau Gasol stayed healthy and led the team in scoring and rebounding.

MORE GO-TO GUYS

Gail Goodrich — 6' 1" Guard
Born: 4/23/1943
Played for Team: 1965–68 & 1970–76
Gail Goodrich played much of his career in the shadow of brighter stars. However, on L.A.'s record-smashing 1971–72 team, Goodrich was the leading scorer. He averaged 25.9 points a game that season.

Happy Hairston — 6' 7" Forward
Born: 5/31/1942
Died: 5/1/2001
Played for Team: 196970 to 197475
Harold "Happy" Hairston was a rebounding machine. He once had 13 defensive rebounds in one quarter. Los Angeles fans were pleased the team traded for Happy. The Lakers went to the NBA Finals three times after he joined the team.

Jamaal Wilkes — 6' 6" Forward
Born: 5/2/1953
Played for Team: 1977–78 to 1985–86
Jamaal Wilkes was nicknamed "Silk" because of his smooth moves on the court. He averaged 20 points a game three years in a row for the Lakers. Off the court, Wilkes was smooth enough to earn roles in movies, television shows, and commercials.

A.C. Green — 6' 9" Forward
Born: 10/3/1963
Played for Team: 198586 to 199293 & 199900
A.C. Green led the Lakers in rebounding six times. His defense helped L.A. Win back-to-back championships in 1987 and 1988.

MORE FUN FACTS

FIRST & FOREMOST
In 1987–88, the Lakers traded for Mychal Thompson, who had been the first pick in the NBA Draft in 1978. That gave L.A. four players who had been the #1 overall pick—Kareem Abdul-Jabbar (1969), Magic Johnson (1979), James Worthy (1982), and Thompson (1978). The Lakers defeated the Celtics that season to win the NBA title.

and click on the tab: **TEAM SPIRIT** to access **FAST BREAK**.

Read all the books in the series to learn more about professional sports. For a complete listing of the baseball, basketball, football, and hockey teams in the **TEAM SPIRIT** series, visit our website at:

www.norwoodhousepress.com/library.aspx

On the Road

BROOKLYN NETS
620 Atlantic Avenue
Brooklyn, New York 11217
718-933-3000
www.brooklynnets.com

NAISMITH MEMORIAL BASKETBALL HALL OF FAME
1000 West Columbus Avenue
Springfield, Massachusetts 01105
877-4HOOPLA
www.hoophall.com

On the Bookshelf

To learn more about the sport of basketball, look for these books at your library or bookstore:

- Doeden, Matt. *Basketball Legends In the Making*. North Mankato, Minnesota: Capstone Press, 2014.
- Rappaport, Ken. *Basketball's Top 10 Slam Dunkers*. Berkeley Heights, New Jersey: Enslow Publishers, 2013.
- Silverman, Drew. *The NBA Finals*. Minneapolis, Minnesota: ABDO Group, 2013.

Index

PAGE NUMBERS IN **BOLD** REFER TO ILLUSTRATIONS.

THE TEAM

MARK STEWART has written more than 40 books on basketball, and over 150 sports books for kids. He grew up in New York City during the 1960s rooting for the Knicks and Nets, and was lucky enough to meet many of the stars of those teams. Mark comes from a family of writers. His grandfather was Sunday Editor of *The New York Times* and his mother was Articles Editor of *The Ladies' Home Journal* and *McCall's*. Mark has profiled hundreds of athletes over the last 20 years. He has also written several books about his native New York, and New Jersey, his home today. Mark is a graduate of Duke University, with a degree in History. He lives with his daughters and wife Sarah overlooking Sandy Hook, New Jersey.